The
Road to Freedom

ADRIANE KROSS

ISBN: 978-1-64570-185-9   (Paperback Edition)
ISBN: 978-1-64570-186-6   (Hardcover Edition)
ISBN: 978-1-64570-184-2   (E-book Edition)

Some characters and events in this book are fictitious. Any similarity to real persons, living or dead, is coincidental and not intended by the author.

Book Ordering Information

Phone Number: 347-901-4929 or 347-901-4920
Email: info@globalsummithouse.com
Global Summit House
www.globalsummithouse.com

Printed in the United States of America

Dedication

I DEDICATE THIS BOOK TO all the people who believed in me and helped me, especially my Healer Keith. To my other healer friend, Bangalore, thank you for your patience.

Also to my friends who had understanding who were affected by this book over the span of twelve and one half years and to all those who turned their heads out of disbelief and greed, they too have their place.

Preface

WE OFTEN ASK OURSELVES, how we arrived here? There is an explanation for everything. The character Mary got to the bottom of the whys and how's, with much bewilderment and fortitude. The characters who gave Mary an awakening brought forth their own interests also. On this long road to freedom, she encountered many obstacles and emotions. Charles our other main character, played the role of facilitator.

He brought Mary to a point of renewed and greater strength, even if it was by unknown means.

Contents

Dedication v

Preface vii

Chapter 1:   Introduction of Characters 1

Chapter 2:   Mary's Encounter with Charles 6

Chapter 3:   Past Lives and Rules 10

Chapter 4:   Fears and Vibration 14

Chapter 5:   Slimy Characters 18

Chapter 6:   Unusual Beings 23

Chapter 7:   Who is in Control? 28

Chapter 8:   Charles's World 33

Chapter 9:   Wanting to be Free 37

Chapter 10: Kenneth and Friends 49

Chapter 11: Shamans, Wise Man and Charles 55

Chapter 12: Love has a Price 65

Chapter 13: Charles's Spoof on Life 68

Chapter 14: Mary's Allegiance 72

Chapter 15: The Battle Waged on 75

Chapter 16: The Creator and Mary 80

Chapter 17: Charles's Tricks 83

Chapter 18: At a Crossroad 87

Chapter 19: The Meeting 91

Chapter 20: A Heavenly Court 93

Chapter 21: So Called Friends and Healers 100

Chapter 22: Love at Last 108

Chapter 1

Introduction of Characters

THE VISION OF SEEING the world crack in 2025 was ever present on her mind. The planet between earth and the moon was being studied, especially the gravitational pull at the earth's core, in 2017. No one as of yet discovered what could occur. Yet all one can ever focus on is every moment, from time to time, just like our time continuum in the hereafter. We think of someone in the hereafter and there they appear.

Physicists and scientists tell us that we have multiple layers or parts that we can pursue. Free will is ever present. We choose the path that resonates with our soul, that inner authority, not our ego. We choose the path before our birth.

There is an infinite amount of timelines, yet why do we choose this path? We choose it before we entered this world to learn, grow and open a new doorway to our self. To reach new heights not only for our self but for our family and ancestry.

As we lift ourselves, we lift them also. And that can work both ways. Our ancestors wait to see if they can be exonerated by our good deeds.

They are looking for a freedom that they lost. This should be recognized but not permitted for the individual called, "you," is separate from the chances our ancestries received. We may lift them, however, they must not live through us. This all can be cleared by a healer, prayer and help of the Creator.

Energetic bullies try to change our path, at the expense of manipulation and control at cross-roads in our lives. Fear and anxiety is ever present, yet let no one interfere with that idea. We all can master it!

By taking layer upon layer from her existence, Mary was able to discover her true identity and remove her resistance to dark negative entities in pursuit of herself. This took years to unravel, in stages, yet it made her stronger and wiser.

While sleeping, we are our most vulnerable. Energies can be sent to the back of the head called the, "Mouth of God," causing fear and anxiety. Others can enter the dream state through astral travel and manipulate your dreams. This is a Mocking Spirit and an intrusion that one quickly finds closing this door, as essential. Qigong meridians is another point of contention that if not properly closed will make you sick through intrusion of foreign energies, if they decide to do so.

In these times of desperation, prayer, fasting and with much camaraderie, one would wish all were not happening to them. But it happened to Mary. Behind this play there was another actor, and that actor was Charles. As dowsers would react, "someone had to play the villain." Surely, "they," would say this since they were never in similar situations nor would they ever be. Underneath all at a far distance, they only spouted that which they knew from their own limited experience.

Upon meeting Charles, when Mary was moving, she felt an uneasiness at her door. That uneasiness was Charles. Mary should have paid attention to that feeling. She was strong in nature but lacked the protection for what Charles represented. Her vulnerability made her an easy target for Charles to invade. He saw her fears above her head. The God force was letting her know that danger was present. It was also odd that a friend from long ago knew she was in town. Upon arriving, she wanted to meet with Mary. Little did

Mary know that she and Charles's ex-wife were setting her up for doom. They even put a spell on Charles to find another, and thus absconding to North Carolina.

How clever, and Mary took the bait! Mary soaked her existence in the Christ force and her own warrior road. Yet Mary did not really know the force within her. As of yet, this would keep her ever vigilant against evil forces.

Charles represented lack all his life. He surrounded himself with demons and entrenched himself with all that was dark and devious. It was second nature to him. And he knew nothing of the light, but feared it. Charles pursuit of Mary was one of love no matter the cost. He was smitten by an energy unknown to him and that in turn became an attraction that even overwhelmed him and possessed him.

The dark forces in turn, marked him and followed him. And there was no escape. In the 70's, he pledged his soul to the Devil and there was no going back. We can also thank his parents for their contribution.

For they too were of a dark sort. Their abusive nature lasted from childhood into Charles's teens. They brought Charles into the world to create chaos and mayhem.

Charles's family were rogues and charalatans. They were powerful people of the shadow, that took care of themselves and others. Charles's mother was a kind soul. She was considered the little lady from Pasadena. She held around her a smoke screen of demonic influence. And she held parties of an Adam family's descent. The apple did not fall far from the tree!

Chapter 2

Mary's Encounter with Charles

THE PRICE OF LOVE can be great. The path of love can be marked with highs and lows, twists and turns. However, for Charles, his love was a persistent annoyance that became destructive with whoever and with anyone who got between Mary and him.

Mary was trapped in a cocoon after she met Charles. Mary was too powerful to be pulled down by Charles alone. So he asked his illuminati friends in China and Russia to help him. Although in their eyes Charles was a rebel, he was able to convince them that Mary was a threat to humanity. They then became interested. Their help consisted of encircling around Mary a cocoon tunnel, so she would become stuck in time. Mary felt it was a sticky substance like molasses. However, it was a long tunnel that she eventually reached the end of. As Mary analyzed and worked through what had happened, her life had been subdued by Charles and he overturned all that he could, her life and her hope. He also placed knots of evil found behind the washing machine and outside her home. One wondered what they were! All happened in that first meeting.

Looking at the bigger picture, there was a demon on the other side orchestrating all. The God force in the other realm allowed this in order for Mary to know who really was in charge. She was to seek the God force and there was no other. Mary soon realized that this road was one of a kind. She decided to shut down her gifts for fear they would be taken, and rightly so.

Charles felt rejection from Mary's reaction, that he could not bear. Dowsers and many healers stated that Mary set this life up before she came to learn lessons, but this was much more than that. Her life evolved as a warrior. And at first she felt she wanted no part of all this nonsense from a person who had an infatuation. If she only knew Charles was a prelude to events about to occur. Staying in the higher realms was not always easy. In so doing, the dark cannot touch you. However, Charles and his assistant reached to higher realms and anchored themselves, always being alerted when monies or when Mary's true soul mate would be approaching. Charles was a principality of dark domain that was filed under the category of black magician, Luciferian, voodoo and of the dark arts.

The pain of rejection at Mary's door, felt by Charles, was greater than he could bear. "If I cannot have her, no one can," he shouted to himself. That vigilant pursuit of someone keeps the soul ever strong and feeling that, "maybe if I continue to wear her down, then I have something to live for." And so he retreated to do just that. He continued on that road to block all she pursued daily, from every level, and he could think of nothing else. He worked in the shadows through mind control and remote viewing. If he could not succeed he would pay others to do unheard of things that would terrorize Godzilla. Yet Mary looked at these circumstances as a cry for love and jumped over these hurdles with not too much frustration.

Mary was slow to anger, quick to love and that was her thumbprint! Yet when her cycle of life was interrupted by her molasses tunnel, her rhythm of life became slower. Over time this became apparent. When Mary did not make a decision fast enough, the moment of indecision was made for her and not to Mary's liking. This created an imbalance that was well received by Charles.

She exemplified to others, a higher consciousness, who sought to remove her past and remove all that was obstructing her path. Her lack of understanding led her on many roads to find answers, to uncover truths and hidden knowledge. Mary's existence never belonged to this world, or so she thought. Her ups and downs in life, created by others, made her uncertain. Yet her certainty of a higher power never faltered.

It is through our light, love and forgiveness that we are heard, no matter what happens to us. And we are able to free that which tries to control us. Our humbleness to say thank you for all that we have each day, is always being heard.

Chapter 3

Past Lives and Rules

MARY NEVER BELIEVED IN past lives yet when Charles used traits of past ancestry found in our DNA, Mary had to resolve past life issues through prayer and past life regression. The ripples of old energy are still ever present within us. Until issues of our past lives are resolved, we are destined to repeat them.

We can be anyone we want to be as long as we follow the rules of life and even in other realms. Even in the Underworld there are rules. And Charles never followed any. Many a time he would take certain aspects of people he didn't like and leave them in the Underworld. Mary rescued a few and much bargaining needed to be done. And the risk was great!

Even Mary from time to time, needed to be rescued from the Underworld. For a price, few ventured to such a feat! Charles would be right there to stop such endeavors. Yet Mary was freed. Those brave souls were handsomely paid who rescued her.

Two particular circumstances stood out in Mary's mind. Charles locked Mary in a room where all eyes were upon her. Another time she was tied to a post and aspects or characteristics of her, were stripped from her. Many soul retrievals took place after this happening.

There were also many for whom Mary trusted, yet would give false information. For this, Mary kept one eye open with discretion and a second opinion was gained. Sometimes the answer did not come easily. One part appeared resolved, while another took its place.

Mary's connection to the God force was also continually blocked by a golden cage. A cage at a higher realm that was kept over her so she would think she were hearing God's voice but in reality she was rewarded by someone else. Mary wondered where people think of these things. Is this knowledge whispered to them by dark demons or passed on to them through their lineage? Some follow the infamous book the Necronomicon, as Charles did. Charles carried it around as if it were his Bible. Before Mary had seen Charles, Mary had a dream. In this dream there was a choice, stay in the room with her parents or go and greet the three monks at the top of the stairs. She chose the monks at the top of the stairs. As the monks took off their hoods, there appeared a young Jesus, a young St. Germaine and a young Merlin. She could not see fully St. Germaine, yet all embraced her. All were a part of her and thus her journey began. They were all there to be called upon if needed and they did so willingly.

From that point, Mary had seen and had been helped by other Archangels who had sealed and protected her from many misfortunes thrown her way. It was upon seeing Archangel Ezekiel, that he came to seal her doors and windows from darkness. He was dressed as a policeman so as to not frighten her. Sometimes we are given sight and thus we truly believe they exist. And, was this only by accident, or was it? Otherwise, how could our faith be tested?

We are all entitled to renewal, happiness and wholeness. When the angels and Archangels did not respond, this made Mary feel unloved and abandoned. No one should have to endure suffering. The sins of our fathers could possibly hold true through this suffering. All is in our DNA!

It is the ah-ha moment, that point of discovery that we are truly aware, not only of seeing a greater picture, but how you resonate as a piece of the whole. And it is at that moment Mary felt at one with herself and at peace with the Creator.

Chapter 4

Fears and Vibration

NO MATTER WHAT CHARLES or anyone did to Mary, her great confidence in those that supported her and her faith, was enough to feel loved and secure.

Mary would find Charles and his entourage would travel to the fourth dimension. Sometimes they would get stuck there, yet Mary would find people who would remove them with ease. Their push and pull caused nose bleeds that sent Mary to emergency. All doorways, portals and tears in the spiritual world would be healed. When Charles became desperate he would open this portal and let all demonic forces descend on Mary. Mary was ready to defend her family, her soul mate and herself. Charles would also create portals in Mary's house and shadows would roam outside that could be caught by the glimpse of your eye. At one time or another, Charles would send a Nephilim to scare her. Mary didn't believe in such things and brushed it off, as though it were an illusion or figment of her imagination. But one day, Mary was reading that a Nephilim with a long red beard was found in Afghanistan and was captured. Mary sat in a room quietly contemplating this thought.

Our intent is very powerful. Whatever our intent projects, it will manifest. It is the power of our mind and our will that overrides adversity. Yet it is our strong faith in whatever or whoever allows us to stand on the conviction of those beliefs, inside of ourselves, that makes us strong. We also need to overcome our fears. Our fears play a large role in this manifestation. As we face our fears we need not experience them again. Charles would enter Mary through a fear found in the subconscious and the spine.

We are all divine, looking from a broader perspective. Even the negative, lower or higher vibrations are just a different vibration of different stages of consciousness. It is the same story for all of us on this planet. All the same but different frequency. And it is all about experiences. We live in a polarity universe, good and bad, black and white and shades of grey in-between.

From the divine perspective there is only conscious and unconscious. And we are becoming more conscious by waking up to our existence and being, fact or fiction.

Most of all, Mary preferred to move to a higher vibration through meditation, prayer and supplication, while her friends were content with their own stance, one of indifference or stagnation. They had their own opinions about Mary that they kept to themselves. Mary appeared as a complex being that had many questionable ideas and thoughts that proved to be too complex for their minds to comprehend. And Mary liked this.

We have gifts to share with the world, to make it a better place, despite challenges. And Mary had not yet reached Mt. Everest, to marvel at greatness within her and say she finally arrived. An Angel whispered to her, "listen to the messages behind the experiences that you have, that is what is important."

Mary was a blessing in anyone's life with a tremendous level of fiery joy. She had a magnetic personality who attracted those connected to nature and with those who desired to create an exceptional life. Mary was funny, caring and dedicated. She was a doctor to our souls and a nurse who provided spiritual aid. Charles saw her as a female who was nurturing and energetic, playing a matron like role in his life. And Mary was all of this and more. She was the type of person who others went to for advice. Mary learned, the more she practiced listening, the stronger her intuition and connection would be to others. Her patience and practical generosity was able thus to recognize negativity as being what it is, not worth her time. Mary was still here in the physical so she could not be considered perfect. Without the dark, the light could not exist.

Chapter 5

Slimy Characters

CHARLES CONNECTED TO THOSE who he tried to control. Those slippery slime that swindled unsuspecting souls. Those rogues of charlatans that were cloaked with unfamiliar grins who turned on anyone that sparked a lending ear. To all who spoke of deals and done deals. Yet they rumbled in dark foreboding places and survive because their space brings balance to the light or so they say. Yet these shadows have never learned to lie flat and learn their misgivings. Those scoundrels! Wave your hands, be gone to dust! For they do not deserve mention except in one act plays that are shuffled out, as cameo appearances disappear!

Charles was part of an alien race as Mary had been, but from different galaxies, from long ago. The distant planet of negativity that he associated with was far away and very cold. He drew strength from this. Mary was from the Orion galaxy and so was her soul mate. Mary's children however were from the Octurion galaxy. Each generation has their spiritual makeup. Races who have implanted land mines within us had to be removed from Mary, just in case he decided to access their place within her. After Mary had these grids removed, no alien race could track her. She wished all could have this done. Maybe this will happen someday.

Charles thought Mary was naïve but never as smart as he, especially in any endeavor. Mary was aware of this and never was boastful. Out of preservation of all she thought was dear, her mind kept it hidden. This was most unfortunate since Charles could read thoughts and project himself in back of Mary, through a holograph. He would listen to her every word and interject what he wanted. His motes operandi would disappear for weeks or months and then pounce on all you thought was dear. His main objective was to wear her down by constant attack and hope that she would give up. Like a dog who remembers where he buried his bone.

Many stood by and didn't help. And they couldn't for fear that Mary would be much more powerful than them. This was very insightful, for the real healer never turns their back nor charges an exorbitant amount of monies, in such circumstances.

Others would retort, "it is cleaning up of your karma, taking back your power and standing your truth no matter what was required. A strong adversary who forced you to do the work and get it done as painful as it was, therefore he was your greatest teacher." Mary wondered if Hitler was a lesson for the world or just plain suffering to endure by the evil one behind him?

Mary was ever vigilant of Charles's schemes. Angels were sent to prevent disasters from happening as do with all of us if we listen and are aware. Angels also disguise themselves so that you are not too alarmed. The Creator was well aware and no plot would ever flourish. For the Creator sought Mary's obedience and acknowledgement.

How Charles, together with his assistant, tried to plot accidents, devious strategies and diabolic schemes, but all would fail, except for a few. Not all was easy. However, a daily vigilance led Mary to be ever watchful and aware.

What are all the vulnerabilities of mankind that allow beasts in? For they are hidden and may appear on other dimensions. And our evolution has not yet accepted that this occurs or has it fully? We evolve by removing and acknowledging our vulnerabilities and particular aspects that keep ourselves prisoner and hold ourselves back as a society. We act as a race of one. Past, present and future are affected by our DNA and genetic structure, which in turn we pass on to future generations. And Mary asked herself if Charles played a part in her evolution? Hidden aspects, once removed energetically, allow us less vulnerability and frees our soul.

Mary received her answers from her angels, meditation and through her dreams. She was also assisted by her healer. We all need an earthly voice to pinch us from time to time and keep us grounded. We need to confide in others for self-acknowledgement. "It is not enough to shield oneself," Mary thought. Many aspects of ourselves need to be changed, removed and modified. It is within that can be touched and not always from without. Mary remembered that if the collective consciousness believes it to be so, then so shall it be. It is the voice of one that can show the way. Mary was guided by one voice, and this voice kept her forever asking and seeking the light. And for this she was thankful and humble. For Charles played as her teacher, her counterpart, helping her grow and dig deep toward understanding, even if pain, loneliness and anger pursued and even if Mary did not understand this at the time.

For those that cause us the greatest pain and suffering in our lives, Mary felt forgiveness was the hardest. Mary could not rise above this suffering and the God force did not respond.

Chapter 6

••••——————————————————————••••

Unusual Beings

A S A RESULT, MARY went on a spiritual journey looking for answers. For God does not want us to suffer. This suffering could go back and forth until a solution is found. And finally one arrived. When the Creator is feared and followed completely, then Mary finally came to know the God force. She realized the Creator was in charge and not Charles. A long unanswered question was finally answered by the Divine. Sometimes we wait a very long time before the divine answers. And when the answer comes, all is in place and the pieces are understood. All is well and then your existence is at peace. The alignment is acknowledged, "I am here and I am heard."

In the back of Mary's mind, Mary wondered if all this time she was a torch of light to be passed on to another. Like the Olympian Games, Mary knew in a moment of time, her mission was consecrated. Mary was anchored in the light despite the endurance of the dark for many, many years and beyond. To be free of the dark is the greatest experience she would ever know. That one day the shadow would no longer blot out her light.

Charles knew instinctively that point in the body that would hit the anger within her. The point of doing this caused disruption and a chaotic tendency to disrupt all those around her. It is at this point Mary was able to contain her emotions and not be too disgruntled.

The Reptilians, the demons and others were relentless behind Charles. Their portals are deep in the ground and mountains. They were wanting Mary to be pushed down. "Her voice would echo her light and that would and should not be permitted," they thought.

Reptilians, these ugly beasts, demand attention. Who knows how many lives they have touched and for that matter have eaten?

Where have they come from? Mary saw one Reptilian out of the corner of her eye. Their 10ft stature was one to behold. David Icke speaks of them, yet his role is to tell their story. And for this Mary was grateful. And Mary was also grateful that there were powerful positive forces keeping Earth in check. It was once said the Annunaki keep a grid around our planet. What would we do if they decided to lift it?

On another level, those from middle earth came to Mary's defense. Those tall beings with red yarn or string around their stomachs. They came around the year 2012 to show their tribute to the United States and how we are all united. The being who stood out of all of this was a tall being who shape shifted and tried to make Mary laugh. Mary was so astonished that she was just amazed about where this being came from and what made her special for them to help her? For whatever reason they did and Mary was glad or so she thought.

Powers on other dimensions, from other galaxies, helped Mary. All she had to do was call out to them. Occasionally the Arcturians and Pleiadians were called upon only when Mary did not feel others were helping her. However, the God force always listens and hears. We have to remember to ask.

The being who accompanied Mary on her journey was rarely called upon. Although Mary acknowledged her presence, Mary felt she could do everything on her own. Charles had systematically planted on Mary's timeline, obstacle after obstacle. On occasion there were even explosions and bombs of energy that went off at precisely the right moment, that were implanted much further in time. A day to day watch was made to avoid these pitfalls and others helped also.

Charles thought it was he alone that made things happen, however it was quite the opposite. He was the puppet for all those of the dark who wanted to carry out their deeds upon humanity. Thousands were affected over time. They knew not what hit them!

Charles could never quite reach the light. He would shy away whenever the light was even mentioned. He in turn thought that if he blotted out Mary with darkness, witchcraft, black magic, sorcery and voodoo, Mary would turn to the Dark side. She would come willingly for his assistance to free her or explain to her what all was happening.

But this never happened, nor would it ever happen. Many soul retrievals occurred after Mary was violated at certain points within her body. Yet Mary never gave up her faith. The Creator knew what she had endured and allowed it. However she was rescued and survived. Her faith alone endured.

It was a game to Charles. And at these junctions, Mary felt a need to call upon her accompanied companion for assistance. A companion who listened to her, in the spirit world. Her healer also helped who held powers Mary did not possess.

Charles would also form groups that would seek his advice on how to do evil. Unbeknownst to these naïve youths, he would corrupt them, then take their energy, as he fled. This occurred over and over again.

The infamous Charles tried to change, detour, all that was directed toward Mary. As though he were an unstoppable God who could not be stopped. And who was going to stop him? Only the Creator could, if he decided to do so.

Chapter 7

Who is in Control?

A YOUNG WOMAN APPROACHED MARY and told her that she was the daughter of Hades. Mary secretly wondered if this woman was making fun of her. Nevertheless, the young woman proceeded to tell Mary that she could see her situation and she would take care of Charles. Mary superficially allowed her to do so. She swallowed Charles whole and then spit him out. Charles wondered what had happened. To this day, he never knew what occurred. Yet Mary laughed and found humor in such an event.

One can go on with their life and never know that an unsuspecting entity has been controlling your life all along. Except in Mary's case, she was an empath and noted and wondered all that was being done to her. Your memories of your youth are there to keep you aware of who you really are and no one can take that away from you.

Maybe we truly are part of a matrix controlled by aliens or with some humor, our government?

Mary thought that it is a reminder to us all that our past patterns of abuse, vulnerabilities or weaknesses need to be removed and acknowledged so they are not repeated in our future. And no one like Charles can control us or attack us through any past or current weaknesses or aspects. All we need to do is have someone check what vulnerabilities and aspects are within and remove them.

The matter of someone entering your subconscious is quite a different matter. Who would know how to do such things? When Mary had a question about someone, her grandmother would comment, "where do you find these people?" Mary wondered herself how people were attracted to her. She knew them all from another lifetime. We all know everyone we meet from the other side. We have contracts to meet them here on earth in one form or another. Did we learn to resolve them?

Charles would try to enter her subconscious mainly while she was asleep, when we are most vulnerable. He would plant anxiety and his assistant would travel to higher realms to plant their attachment to each other, from above so below. Any frustration or confusion on Mary's part resulted in an attachment by Charles. Emotions, fear and trauma all play a part of attachment. The actual portal, entrance, grid or hole just needs to be sealed. Beware of eating or spending monies with no forethought. Someone may be playing on your vices.

Honorable mention also lead Mary to remember, through qigong points at night, portals or entrances to organs, can be accessed. This left her in a weakened state. The implant of various entities could also occur. Mary was left in bewilderment as to what needed to be removed. In a weakened state, if not corrected soon, the body would become very weak and disoriented. At times Mary would also receive Reiki treatments, being that she was a master in Reiki. However sometimes Reiki left a vulnerability that allowed Charles to enter Mary easily. Charles had meshed his soul with Mary's and it was very difficult to pry him loose, a soul tie.

Mary's ascension became more pronounced and the turning point in her life had begun. There is a point where Mary was striving for higher and higher realms as Charles was continually attacking her body and soul. There is a point in anyone's life that you either give up or go beyond to raise yourself higher. Mary crossed that threshold and vowed to herself that no one would do these things to her, especially when nothing was done to Charles. He retaliated in such an aggressive manner! He would pull her in a direction she did not want to go. No one has the right to do this. Mary was not wealthy nor wanting to be wealthy. All Mary ever wanted was to live peaceably with her soul mate, not hurting a soul. And she found herself in a spiritual battle for her life and her soul. The Creator knew what was happening!

As we grow spiritually or learn our lessons in life, we eventually reach the status of Archangel, or at least Mary was told. By reaching that of an Archangel we continue to become part of the God force. Even though many others told her that humans can never be angels or archangels, Mary would always wonder.

A friend asked her not to participate in astral projection. Although Mary had never entered the etheric world, she was curious about this subject. Charles may have accessed this realm. This realm was dangerous. Bad thought forms, and people who have died and were criminals, stayed here. They do not want to go to heaven nor do they want to go to hell. The lower fourth dimension, harbor dark demons. So these demons take hold of those earthly people who enter the etheric realm by astral projection. This is entertainment for these criminals.

September 23rd, 2015 was a monumental date. Cern was able to pierce a small hole in the veil between our world and the lower fourth dimension, where demons live. Since that date, some demons have been able to come through the etheric realm and they will continue to come through. Charles was aware of this and he tried to take hold of this happening.

We on the third dimension, need not worry. However, these demons wait on the fourth lower dimension and anyone doing astral projection will be taken. The demons will make them do terrible things. And Mary was told that anyone who does astral projection will have their life ruined and their family's also. Mary just listened to all that was said for she knew Charles had attempted this and had failed with Mary. Yet Charles would try anything for the thrill and sheer power to overcome it and possess it. He also gathered others' belongings even if they meant nothing to him. He was a collector!

Chapter 8

Charles's World

A LTHOUGH MARY HAD MANY past lives with Charles, all had been distinguished. Many healers feel that there are no past lives, only one life. And Mary thought this too. That is, until Mary was attacked on a past life level, and traits from ancestors were brought forward and projected into Mary. And when Charles did this, many ancestors were shocked and disturbed that this negative being would attempt such a feat. Seeing someone from the earthly world make an attempt to extract something from the deceased, was quite alarming, from both sides.

Guides can be changed. Lifetimes can be switched to other lifetimes. Yet each have a cameo appearance on earth, and in particular the third, fourth and fifth dimension. Even planets and galaxies, can be accessed. We are all ever spinning!

"Let the God-force take care of Charles," many yelled. Yet this battle raged on for many a time times time. No one could stop Charles and no one dare try!

Mary went back constantly to the past when they first met. If only she knew about the court of atonement back then. She would have stated emphatically to reverse the moment she gave up her power and all would have been solved. Yet that day did not arrive. We can reverse our involvement by acknowledging when we gave our power away. And once we remember when this first occurred, we can stop all from occurring as we proceed forward in that very minute. Much more needed to be done. And yet this method did not help Mary fully.

Charles was a tall wiry figure with thick glasses who looked like Andy Warhol. His gnarly fingers were a result of his evil deeds and all the black magic he had casted upon others. His silence spoke of mysticism and a reverence. Yet one felt pity and a sense of loneliness that he alone suffered. You see he had a broken heart or heart chakra. This sympathy was played upon well for favors rendered by his relatives and others.

Charles brief encounter with Mary happened when she was moving. However, he planted a seed deep, deep in her subconscious, that would follow Mary everywhere. She was tracked wherever she went. And this she did not discover for a long time. This happened when he met her.

There was a silence one day that Mary felt. Yet this silence made one wonder what Charles was up to. It was discovered that he had taken a part of her while asleep. By traveling through a qigong point and traveling through her nerve pathway, he was able to hit a part of her heart. From this he took a loving attachment and made it into a dark negative clone. It was projected that Mary would join Charles and the others to live in dark infamy together. Yet Mary's clone never fit in. Mary's healer rescued her from this deep dark clone and Mary was free. What a contrived imagination! What extreme measure was Charles capable of? This proved he was holding onto a dream that Mary would someday be his.

Mary had been very patient in meeting her soul mate. Very patient to rise above the challenges that Charles had made on her path every day. No one would attempt it. If only she knew what awaited her prior to her moving. It was a thought out plan by the Divine to work out and Mary had to solve it. A jigsaw puzzle of Divine order!

One day, Charles was no longer Charles. He was a combination demon, principality, reptilian, black magician and energetic vampire, that he no longer could control. He had been overcome by the darkness, anger and hostility. The dark comes to collect, especially the Underworld when darkness is not paid back. And someday he would pay for his crimes. But that day was not now, nor would it be for some time.

The biggest distortion to Mary was her timeline. Five minutes and fifteen would disappear. And Mary felt her time was being erased. There is such a thing as sewing of time and this is what was happening. Mary had found someone to unravel this sewing and set her free. All that was sealed behind her became free. However, the darkness continued to loom over her.

Mary was reminded of Charles's opinion, "she never would be as smart as he, especially in any endeavor." He began to send curses, and overturning everything on her path, monies, possessions and all that was coming to her. Mary felt helpless at times that only The Creator could hear, yet she never gave up. Only demonic forces overturn all that is good causing chaos, disruption and mayhem. Was this all due to the revenge and rejection in that one hour, one lifetime? No, this was a play and Charles was playing his part by fulfilling his role quite well. Yet at the time he wanted his Mary and felt she would come to him.

Chapter 9

Wanting to be Free

MARY REALIZED HER MISGIVINGS and wanted to take everything back that she had said to Charles, yet Charles replied with a Luciferian energy that penetrated right through her, during a phone call. A streamline energy of pure evil!

Another healer worked with Mary to remove a past life all the way back to the year, 325 B.C. Charles had been accessing this vulnerability. One particular past life was discovered with Charles, that stood out from the six past lives she shared with him. Mary had given over her power in mostly all of them. It was at the time of Atlantis, and Mary had been his younger sister. Mary could reach higher dimensions, similar to this life. In this particular lifetime, he would use her gift unbeknownst to him, similar from the past.

They both followed the snake, Negus, and they paid homage to the serpent. This puzzle piece fit tightly!

In a box, in Mary's earth chakra or in the earth, her healer opened the box using vibrational tones that were finely programmed. No it was not Pandora's Box, but an attachment, a stronghold, that firmly held Mary to repeat lifetime after lifetime with Charles and his comrades. This loop was finally broken, or so Mary thought. Believing in your healer is the first step.

It was stated that Anton Levey called out to Jesus before his death, for mercy. And Mary believed that Charles might do the same. Charles feared the God force but he never knew the light nor did he pay any homage to it. Mary exemplified the light. And in knowing this, Mary forgave him. If Charles loved himself, he would never try to control Mary. His yearning for Mary exemplified his inner drive to search for love that he never received. Even his mother used him yet he loved her in a different manner. His soul's insistence for control empowered him. And for this no one could fully embrace him with love. Besides, he would torture them!

Mary realized that humanity needs to be armed spiritually. There are few souls who are protected spiritually from all and Mary met a few. There are strict rules that govern the hereafter. No matter in which direction you are directed to, Charles knew all of them and followed none of them. He was a rebel that felt himself untouchable. That is until the moment when the Creator intercedes or as the old fable mentions, when Icarus gets too close to the sun and falls from the sky.

Prayer and keeping to her ever vigilant routine toward the light would save Mary. And for Mary, her fight for survival would be a struggle. United we stand was filtering through her mind like a wandering river. And yet those false healers reverberated, in her thoughts, "false imposters." They were colored green with a veneer of ugly tar that one would never want to encounter again, nor look at. Mary's fight was hers alone and she was not going to run from it. Her feet were imbedded in quick sand and she needed to pull herself from it.

Spirit has a way of finding you. Through other family members, the dark can enter their bodies through arguing or friction with others. Charles would cause disruption between Mary's son and her. Once the spark would fly, the energy would transfer from her son to her. It became a revolving wheel that needed to be stopped. When we do not understand the unknown, we immediately go to fear and like the turtle, bury ourselves in our shell. Charles entered through the subconscious and thus manipulated her son. That is why it is important to always treat the whole family in any disease and for that matter any attack!

Charles and the others would also take Mary's son's energy through his subconscious while sleeping. They left him in a state of emptiness and created a young man not being able to bridge youth with maturity. By taking the good energy, Charles was able to control him by using mind control and working through the subconscious. It is at this state that Charles was able to abuse Mary by inflicting male abuse through her son. For then she not only had to contend with Charles, she also had her son delivering verbal abuse. Mary understood this but not her son.

Every time her son went for a job, the subconscious was targeted by Charles. He interjected a high degree of anxiety and fear of making decisions. Charles and his comrades also energetically bridged the gap between Mary's soulmate and her son by placing her son in that position. In this manner, the placement was fulfilled and no soulmate could fill it. The rejection of women was also planted at certain junctures so that her son could not have a girlfriend or loved one without friction. And this also occurred at any prospective job. The main concern for Mary was not to find her soul mate but also Charles did not want her son bringing any monies to his mother also. The voice of abuse was great and it rang loudly at Mary's household!

Once Mary discovered the cues to how the anger would rise, she quietly and quickly, became the turtle and would not allow it to fester.

The veil of cloaking can be mastered but this takes time. If only Mary could make Charles see that her refusal to be his friend was rooted in fear and nothing more.

When no one is there to turn to, we are forced to turn to the God force and rightly so. We are then reminded of who we are and why we are here. We come to raise our vibration no matter how low and grow as human beings. Mary was told by a seer that the planet Earth is the only planet with humans on it. All other beings reside on the fourth dimension or higher, etheric dimensions, although aliens are among us. No, there are other beings on other planets. Kepler-444 hints at the existence of other planetary systems and possible life inhabitance. On all sides of Mary, Charles would daily watch her every move. Since he was able to access her timeline, he would negate any male on her path. Our path is a culmination of circles. This is our timeline, we travel in circles. Mary wondered if he could read her DNA?

Any job or situation which seemed threatening to his love for her, would be thwarted. He would go on her timeline and negate it, and change her path. And in turn Mary would become lonelier and pray more. Until Prayer became a vigil day and night and many vibrational tones were sung. It was the only way to clear any negative energy sent to her. Her soul mate was ever present in the foreground, however he never appeared. Even if Mary did not even like Charles and he knowing this, he would pursue her just the same. He loved her no matter if she would never love him. And it is hard to say if Charles would ever know the meaning of that word. He never wanted anyone to love her, except him. His love turned to anger, frustration, then rage!

Each day, Mary spoke of clearing chords between her and Charles on all levels. Archangel Michael helped with this act. And each day she pleaded with the Creator to free her and forgive her and her ancestry, for anything they may have done. Yet the battle waged on. The revenge of rejection weighed heavily on Charles's mind. The anger festered to his higher self that at times exploded when Mary closed all doors to his intrusion.

The rampage of his anger was fueled by not wanting Mary to win. Win what? He wanted her to give in to his powers and all Mary wanted was to be free. But Charles could only see his own vision. If Mary were about to be freed, Charles tried harder to block, destroy and negate all in Mary's life. Mary knowing this, never challenged Charles. Maybe she should have!

Challenging Charles would mean there was a battle when in reality no battle existed at all. Just the right to be free from oppression, negativity and darkness was her divine right always. And Charles would be no exception. No one has that right to condemn us nor keep us prisoner. Everyone is free to be who they want to be! The scratchy and heavy energy that Charles left was always felt by Mary.

Charles's consciousness held 3 fragments that were controlled by female dark forces. These 3 fragments of female origin were creating division between female and male energies within Mary. These energies traveled through the earth chakra and up into Mary's legs. These energies were very slippery.

Their names were Vela, Kashonda, Eloisa, Luchendi and Mysteries of the Darkness. Dissipating energies were initiated by her healer from a high level. It was then found that the 3 fragments of Charles were connected to deeper forces in deeper layers. Archangel Michael was called in to initiate and remove these dark feminine forces.

Charles knew that these forces created division within the masculine and feminine in Mary. As time would pass, the feminine would not trust the masculine in Mary, and vice versa. Mother Mary was also called in to help Mary also.

These fragmented pieces from Charles were removed and the pieces were taken by the divine so they could no longer hurt anyone. And all energetic cords were cut so no attachment could take hold.

As the energy from Mary's legs traveled upwards, the energy became very heavy around the crown Chakra or head area. Preventing all from the divine was Charles's objective with the dark energies also. As her healer discovered, these dark energies had integrated into her back. They were also busy creating a different path for Mary to follow. Mary's healer was able to dissipate all and remain stable. Thank the divine for such a healer as this. Mary's timeline would also be disrupted if this was not corrected and thus Mary would not meet her soulmate. This energy that ran through Mary's back was karmic. Old karmic life impressions were seen that were integrated from the past. These forces were of a dark nature. Although we walk away from dark forces, once integrated in our past, through our ancestry, it does not necessarily let us go. Dark forces were holding onto the male and female energy from within. Energies were brought in. A new higher realm between Mary and her soul mate were intertwined. Restoration energies were then integrated. All was done by her healer. These forces created chaos and confusion thus causing a hold on her timeline. However, they too were released from a higher vibration when introduced. These forces were also integrated into the chakras held together by a mechanism that called back these fragments. All were eventually released. We are complicated individuals, yet Charles complicated the situation with deeper ideas to imprison Mary. Mary felt like a new person once they were removed.

You see when Charles would not get a response from Mary that he wanted, he would be forever plotting against her. He decided to split Mary in two using a stake through the masculine, and his Shaman friend placed a stake through her feminine part. This caused a great division in Mary that he could take advantage of on many levels. Much healing was needed to bring these parts back together as a whole. Once a division is made with the right and left side of the body, each representing the feminine and masculine, on the etheric level, division on all levels takes place. Thus, this division creates a split between love, monies and many more divisions unspeakable. The balance between financial security and self-affirmation was disturbed. An opening is easily accessible mostly through spiritual, emotional and physical layers surrounding us. The retaliation by Mary was fueled by rising ahead of Charles. Mary was at the top of his Adriane messenger list that he visited daily, to bother herself and others. Mary never challenged Charles, she just wanted to be free. Asperger's Syndrome, one of Charles's characteristics, exemplified his eagerness to win, to dominate. Mary was fighting for her life. A Legion and followers of Charles tried to push her down and subdue her. No one goes unscathed under those dark forces, let alone are permitted to live. Yet Mary continued onward and at times her physical strength would falter.

At one point she lost her job, fell out of a car and fell down stairs. This resulted in fracturing her shoulder, breaking her leg and suffering trauma, all in three days. An accumulation of dark forces reached a pinnacle of destruction and were released. As these forces were thrust at Mary, they fell down from above upon her into the physical. The form took place in the higher realms and then took form in the earthly. A healer once cleared Mary on all layers and for some reason did not clear all. The tipping point occurred and Mary's accident resulted.

Charles also manipulated neighbors and tried very hard to place Mary in positions of abuse that were rendered. In this manner, Charles could work through others to verbally abuse and belittle her. Mary knew his schemes and was ever ready to meet them with vigor and strength. Yet these vulnerabilities and weaknesses persisted

And Charles was able to enter her body and soul. It was very hard at times for Mary to be kind and understanding toward Charles. Mary would react by saying to herself he was not well or he does not know what he is doing. However, his actions spoke otherwise. And in that first 1 hour of meeting, Mary remembered Charles stating, "I never lose a battle nor do I win." Mary would never see Charles again from that one and only meeting. The scars were felt by Mary and throughout her life, Mary would not forget them. For they were deep and hurtful and never to be repeated. The lessons of discrimination were well learned!

"The innocent will have their hands full," as the saying goes. Innocent because Mary would expect miracles. Hands full because any miracle would fill Mary with joy. And there were quite a few that happened along the way.

The mere handshake of a stranger took away her light. Anyone could have made that mistake. Mary learned from her mistakes and looked to the future in a new way. A second chance was always in the offering. It was Mary who had to accept this and acknowledge it. It is in this particular climate that you have to make important decisions. Sharing periods of generosity and happiness with people around Mary became foremost. We act on the information that we know and we do the best with that. Even if all the facts are not in plain view. We silently and patiently wait for that moment when all is revealed to us. And sometimes that can be a lifetime.

Chapter 10

Kenneth and Friends

MARY DECIDED TO ENGAGE in quantum jumping. An action that allows you to be in different places at one time. Charles would never find her or so she thought. This lasted for one year and a half. Charles finally found her. Mary also attempted alternate universes however this took much strategic action and Mary was not amused to play Charles's game or games. This male Medusa kept running to and fro and all who looked his way got entangled in his web. It was odd that he wore a male Medusa around his neck to ward off all his enemies. Look who was calling the kettle black!

Charles petitioned the dark forces to grant him favors after explaining Mary's aspirations and goals. They granted his Luciferian wishes. Charles knew that one day the dark forces would come to collect on such favors, whether he succeeded or failed.

Mary knew she had help on her path, as we all do. We can learn to hear and acknowledge our guides. They are placed at birth. Mary had an extra guide that assisted with obstacle after obstacle. All she had to do was know her existence. If we are fortunate, there are others who guide us along our path. Receiving communion, reading the bible, prayer and singing various vibrations all were important to Mary.

Long in finding, Mary encountered a man with thick dark eyebrows and black wavy hair. He was marked on her destiny like Peter Cottontail who meets the farmer. Her questions ranged from, "Is pain the answer to redemption and higher purpose?" No, this was an esoteric war of unprecedented absurdity of a possessed being, a darkness who Mary would not obey.

A healer, named Kenneth, answered, "no matter how much Charles travelled to higher realms and to the depth of your subconscious, it is you who has to guard yourself and then forgive. When our lives are disrupted and for a long time, we rely on our happy memories to bring us back to our happiness of life. Your strength and stubborness in your beliefs allow no one to shake that foundation, being right or wrong. And it is worthy to note that evil souls use past memories or habits in this lifetime or your generational past, to find unhealthy patterns of abuse. In this manner they can work against you. These family patterns can be visited through portals and are cast upon you. And all you have to think of is a past memory." Mary listened in awe, as these words were penetrating her very soul. "The soul is on an infinite journey, far beyond human comprehension," Kenneth spoke. Mary realized that fear broke things down, but love was used to rebuild. "We need to try to access our creative, intellectual, imaginative self. And our past lives are a discovery of these experiences. All past lives are one soul, a reflection of one soul. Everyone we connect with is a reflection of the soul. It is our ego that separates us from our soul," Kenneth stated. Mary conveyed to Kenneth that she agreed with his wisdom. Mary spoke to Kenneth of her own visions and truth. She saw in the future, 2025, a planet coming close to earth and causing a crack. Scientists are studying this now. Kenneth just listened and did not reply. Mary also envisioned the veil to the other side being very thin and "We will be able to communicate with ease to all our loved ones very soon. Today there are certain people who can tune into frequencies. Since everything is vibration, at different levels, scientists will build machines to access this frequency. Mary wondered what it would be like to talk to relatives or Einstein? This energy pattern will be sent to our brains and it will be able to be translated. Mary thought, "maybe people will not be so skeptical of past lives and much more?" Scientists today state that in 2029 and in 2036, asteroids will come close to earth. On earth today, there are many who energetically can push them away. People push hurricanes away, why not asteroids? Kenneth just listened. Kenneth hardly spoke of Charles. Perhaps Kenneth felt a sadness and heartfelt feeling from Mary. He did state before he left, "just keep prayer always knowing that all can be diminished." "Remove all discordant energy chords daily and release it to be transmuted with love by Divine Source, closing all energy doorways and filling them with golden Creator substance for all time. Remove from your record the curses that are currently affecting you. Delete these curses backwards to its lifetime of origin and forwards through seven generations, leaving all learning experiences free from trauma and restrictions. Dissolve and remove from your record any agreements or contracts between yourself and these entities. Return these entities to their appropriate astral plane. Block all access between these entities and you permanently. Fill all memory channels and access points with Divine light. Clear and remove all negative programs and discordant energies associated with these entities."

Mary wondered if Kenneth was accessing her Akashic records, a hall where are past records can be accessed. But Kenneth was only speaking words of wisdom.

After all, Mary had gone through her life searching. She needed change. She began asking herself a lot of questions. Experience is an asset for everyone but sometimes the memories are painful. Old wounds from the past, all that Charles enacted, represented a dark period of her existence. Jealousy from others, especially Charles, rang with a loud cry of disdain. As the years passed, Mary learned to live with these dark memories, the absences and the wounds. Many events Mary could not have been predicted, affected her personally. These knawing doubts resurfaced time and time again. The dawn of change was imminent. Doubt filled her mind about the future. But Mary knew the answer somewhere hidden deeply in the recesses of her inner self. And those on the other side were trying to reach her. For every new beginning Mary attempted, Charles would delete it in order to keep her on his path.

The balance of material and spiritual was always a challenge to Mary. She was autonomous in her way of looking at things. She had a unique vision of the world. Her way of life was marked by many upheavals.

It seems that in the past she was faced with difficult situations that had left wounds that were still felt today. If she follows the right path, makes the right concessions, she would be able to advance enormously. The sense of nostalgia from time to time surfaced when she thought about what she had gone through and what she could have accomplished. Mary often enjoyed thinking about past events, about all those things she shared with the most important people in her life. These nostalgic temperaments, of spiritual and intellectual qualities, lead her to think constantly about her life path, her track record and her future destiny. Mary could not feel or know these experiences fully due to Charles and he did not allow her to grasp her future with more foresight every day. Yet her sacredness evolved. She did know however, that she alone had the power to connect with all those things that really mattered to her. And all that Charles placed upon her made them even more precious. Yet at times, all that Charles did was life threatening and the darkness was ever menacing. Mary needed her family and friends to feel truly happy, but they did not always understand the distress she was under. She did not want to bother them with her problems. Mary felt alone in this manner and that was alright. It is when a new dynamic enters your life that pushes the past in the past.

Chapter 11

Shamans, Wise Man and Charles

MARY LEARNED FROM HER mistakes and was looking to the future in a new way. Every time she was cleared by her healers, a new level was cleared. Although energy from Mary could be followed to all that was dear to her, anyone can call in Arch Angel Michael to cut all chords, threads, darts and arrows on all dimensions and timeframes. It is true that in some situations, life gives us a second chance and always another, that we have to seize. Mary never gave up. But it is always cautious to not proceed in haste. For every new beginning, the healer or Mary initiated, Charles continued to keep ever vigilant to stay one step ahead of her and work in the shadows. What better way to control Mary, hourly and daily!

Mary also realized that some people are very important in your life but are unable to be around, due to life circumstances. This is why you must make the most of the periods of generosity, sharing and happiness that you have with the people around you. These people are given your trust and whose uniqueness gives you everything you need today.

Mary thought of herself as holy yet this darkness was far greater than anything she could imagine. She understood as time went on, that she was a beacon for others to not give up under the guise of adversity.

Mary amazed herself by her strength of endurance that she could emotionally, physically and spiritually uphold. No matter how hard she tried to find her soulmate, who was searching for her, Charles would feed into that yearning and negate that meeting. He attached himself to that emotion. Mary could not explain all that was happening to her. Who would believe her?

Charles knew which tone activations correspond with sadness, depression, anxiety, anger and frustration. Whenever Mary displayed these emotions, he was able to bind her and take hold of her. Each emotion carries a vibration that can be isolated and studied. So Mary was very perceptive to her feelings. Whenever possible she made a notebook full of laughter and joy. And she studied to catch herself when other emotions surfaced, trying to change her patterns. Charles throughout the many lifetimes with Mary, was given permission to have control over her. Mary in other lifetimes allowed this. This factor was not discovered for many years until her healer put an end to it. He also put an end to illusionary and mesmerizing energy. Charles would create illusions by not allowing her to see the truth of what was occurring. As you were mesmerized, an illusionary energy surrounded you. Your energy was focused in that direction. When the whole time, the real drama was happening somewhere else to you.

One day or another, a Shaman decided to put an end to Charles. "These plans have to be executed with great precision," he stated. For Charles would step into the void or fall through a trapped door, already planned in case of an emergency. For many in the past have tried and failed. Their large ego's fell to extinction with a response of, "I can't understand it, it never fails." At the right time and place, this Shaman was able to strip Charles of his physical power. The ego of this Shaman grew like a giant sequoia. All went well until Charles would emerge after all that was said and done. This time what emerged was a darker soul, for this remained. And this was one calculation the Shaman did not take into consideration. The anger of Charles rose like a furnace. What remained of his ancestral energy was passed onto a fellow female Shaman comrade who did not want it but received his energy nevertheless.

Mary in the beginning of combating with Charles sought the help of a female Shaman. Shamans fight the dark. That is their quest! She was helping Mary initially. This female Shaman saw the power Charles possessed and she immediately took up residence with Charles. She then came against Mary. Mary learned a grave lesson that day. Only seek the God force!

Mary also sought the help of an Indian wise man who spoke words of wisdom. The Shaman and Charles attacked the wise man. And the wise man fell from grace. That was something to behold! So at the time of Charles's defeat of his body, all were present to contribute to his soul. From that day, Charles had to seek the energy of the female Shaman, the Indian wise man and he worked through them as the power of one. And this was from the beginning at the time of his downfall, from the male Shaman. These comrades felt they were fighting for their lives once Charles took hold. Their hearts were empty for quite a long time and maybe forever.

Their loyalty to Charles remained for they were threatened with death, otherwise. No matter how hard they tried to escape, Charles would not let them. It is at this point that they realized their misgivings, however it was too late. For whom the bell tolls, it tolls for thee!

Mary's male Shaman friend, disappeared out of site. Mary could not reach him nor find him. His camouflage techniques were very thorough. Yet she felt disappointment in his heart. He tried his best and the god-force knew this.

That unwavering, unstoppable, mighty Charles, was a steam engine with control, abuse and anger in his soul! When he did not reach his mark, he dug deep in the shadows to undermine those who felt they were secure and stable. The Grinch diabolically planned his next move and Mary did not know how to stop him. The tumbleweed ran down the road, as one marble affected the other. The chaos was unmatched by any human. Someone, anyone, throw a silver netting over him! The creator sees all. All from the other side, cheered Mary on. Mary's stubbornness spit in the face of Charles and no matter what Charles threw at her, she got up and dusted herself off.

When these energetic blows would hit Mary's body, they sometimes contained poison. They would push Mary's body in a direction she really did not want to be pushed to. One night, Charles traveled to her bedroom and emitted a poison by her nose. To Mary's surprise she was able to find someone on the internet who could take this poison away from her lungs. At the hospital, nothing was found in her lungs, the poison went undetected. If the man on the internet did not find the poison, she would have gotten very ill. As Charles inflicted negative energies to Mary, her body was regenerating to a new soul. The body knows how to repair itself from the soul over mind and not the other way around. Mary was not only able to preserve herself but also the Creator kept her alive. Mary was busy shutting down her abilities, her aspects and her gifts in order for them to not be stolen. The Tasmanian Devil would plunder, loot and cause chaos with whatever he touched or felt drawn to. His jangled, gnarly fingers, moved the evil he sent. One wondered if Charles loved himself? Sometimes those that do evil try to gain attention to themselves but they never love themselves. Yet in Charles's case, his revenge took on a different meaning. An imagined grievance that took the depth of a shadowy figure who caused lack. His lies kept voicing Mary's injustices of his fractured soul!

Mary would send love to him through the Ho'oponopono prayer. She thought this would disable hatred and anger. A Hawaiian practice of reconciliation and forgiveness. For this action, Charles continued on his ways. Mary had to be careful because sending love to a being who was doing evil could be interpreted as true love. And that was definitely what Mary did not want. Mary's love was sent so that Charles's interpretation could be received as compassion and forgiveness toward her. These emotions were bound with glee. Despite Mary's attempt, he loved her deeply and he excluded himself forever in isolation pinning for her daily, hourly. "No one is for me, except Mary," he whispered to himself. And there was no changing Charles's mind. Past lives, although cleared, reminded Charles that she had given herself over to him to be controlled. And this present life was no different, she discovered. All were from past lives.

Mary was not ready on a spiritual level to let go of Charles. The memory was on her hard drive. She did not take the memories to be transmuted from the low frequencies into high frequency energy essence, as of yet. For Mary looked at Charles as having some good in him. Charles knew this and bound this emotion till it was air tight. For Mary thought there was some good in everyone.

John, Mary's soul mate, on the other hand, was being pulled and thwarted in a different direction away from Mary. Over time, Charles worked on all Mary's family, as he intertwined himself. He felt himself a part of something he hadn't before. Charles needed to be needed, even if it were only in his mind. He whispered to Mary's soulmate. "Do not look for her, or, your relationship makes no sense." Mary's soulmate knew different, yet Charles persisted for a very long time. He did this to wear him down and at times her soulmate was very confused and hatred would set in. Charles found some humor in this. Mary would search for her soul mate. However, she too was pulled to and fro. Charles and his entourage watched her viscerally and diligently. If they per chance could not find Mary, their spell or curse placed a veil over their eyes so they could not see or find one another. Mary was sure they came close to one another a few times but neither would be able to see one another. How sad! Another technique Charles applied was to use mind control on John's family members. By energetically going through John's family, Charles was able to use mind control to pull John away from Mary. Initially, Charles placed Mary and her soul mate in convoluted tubings so that they would miss each other by five minutes. How sad indeed! But what Charles did not know was the fact that John and Mary were of the same thread. And No one could separate them. They were two powerful beacons of the light. They were searching for each other for nine lifetimes!

All three or four comrades would assist Charles in directing John down a dark road. As time passed, John understood what was happening to him and quickly diverted these circumstances to happen. Next, memories of past loves were introduced so John would be led in a different direction. John quickly was able to never go back into the past and correct these matters. Charles worked through others. Charles and his entourage were diligent in their undertakings! Mary was glad her soul mate jumped over those hurdles without too much difficulty, even though he did not know what was happening. If John only knew what was occurring in the shadows, he may have not felt depressed, indifferent and disgruntled. These emotions were bonded by Charles, with glee.

For the truly evil, these are attributes that they prey on. The evil diabolic Charles felt like the Grinch who wielded his ugly nature and that he did for a long time. And his grin got a little wider with each glee. Charles also caused Mary's soulmate to have his feelings buried very deep within him so that he would not be able to express them fully to Mary. Charles could not stand anyone loving Mary other than him. And as time went on, he would whisper and overtake the feeling of love that would turn her soulmate's love for Mary, into hatred and anger.

I suppose in one time or another, Charles would get tired and stop this charade. However, the insane and evil act just the opposite. As the Illuminati profess, "even if it takes generation after generation we will get our point across." Charles would pull back, letting you think he had retreated when at a moment unexpected, he burned brightly right in front of you. It would be at a moment you would least expect. Evil waited, evil consumed and evil marched forward!

Yet Mary never alluded to or succumbed to Charles's deviousness. Mary consulted many to find a solution to all that was happening. And the Creator heard Mary's cries.

Raising her vibration, relieving layers from her soul, compassion, prayer, fasting and keeping a clear head, kept Mary sane and feeling safe. All the time Charles felt pompous and untouchable. Mary would be blocked by a demon on the road to block her daily, while Charles and his minions would do what they had to do in order to refute, dismantle and negate all that was coming to Mary. Charles as a trademark, would leave a demon on Mary's path, at every juncture, she wanted to go. It was his calling card!

Chapter 12
_____

Love has a Price

ALL THE REMOTE VIEWERS that Mary consulted were not of any help. After much consternation, monies and confusion, Mary could not find John. At times, Mary had so much done to her that all she could do is pray day and night. When all roads are closed, prayer was the only solution.

In Charles's eyes, only Mary and he, were one. And Charles tried to accomplish this, when genetically his Asperger's Syndrome could only experience his feelings, no one else's. Yet when he and Mary first said hello, they had never again conversed, nor would they ever. This revolving loop continued till one would win over the other. It came to Charles one day, as years went by, that Mary never really loved him. Despite all this, he continued his pursuit, just in hopes that she would change her mind. And his male abuse, control and diminishing control over any good fortune that came Mary's way, continued. His jealousy overpowered him. His intertwining amongst Mary's family continued so that he felt he controlled her family at will. Mary was busy feeling angst and disheartened emotions for all that was happening. Each time she detected this about to happen, she smudged, prayed and placed brick shavings around all doors and windows. Calling in Jesus, Archangels and all who would listen, was done also.

If Mary tried to meet someone or consult with police or friends, all actions were blocked by Charles. His monitoring her actions were quite diligent and precise. Mary contacted the FBI, CIA and Homeland Security anonymously. However no response was ever returned. Charles had blocked all.

Mary at times felt she was living on the dark side of the moon. Charles would also pierce through Mary's higher realms, which enabled him to catch all the good that Mary was to receive. Mary always placed her full armor around all she loved. "Never lose hope, never give up and never stop believing in yourself," she told herself. "No matter how difficult the path and where it will lead you."

Upon shaking hands with Charles, her light would be taken. He would look above her head and see all her fears. This was his control upon her and thus he could analyze all that he needed to know about her. We hold our blueprint four feet above our heads. Chording or energy attachment, instantly took place between Charles and Mary, and with anyone he knew or met.

Mary consulted with a so called holy woman, upon first meeting Charles. She overlooked Charles and unbeknownst to Mary, dismantled his coven in a matter of less than five minutes. "There, that should help you." Mary never heard from her again nor did she remember her name.

Mary's angels and guides reminded her that, "justice clearly reminds us that the balance between positive and negative elements is always precarious, and therefore your situation will always have highs and lows. "Don't worry too much about it and concentrate on the little things that give you moments of happiness." We all need to listen to that small voice within us when it is trying to speak to us.

Chapter 13

Charles's Spoof on Life

S PIRIT TRIES TO TALK to us through our dreams. Charles and his students would enter her dreams through an astral fracture and manipulate them towards the negative. His students would take them, taint them and then throw them at unsuspecting children so they would experience nightmares. One time they even pushed Mary aside in the dream state and took a group picture of themselves. Such egos! From this point on, Mary was fearful of going to sleep. Prayers were said.

There are others also who upon seeing you feel you are vulnerable and try to perform their powers by moving you while asleep. Unsuspecting youths with pickup trucks who test their abilities, only caring about themselves. Mary would know who they were and would be well guarded while asleep. Is this what happens when youths are bored with life?

There are holes in the earth that Charles would visit to bring healing to himself, whenever he was in battle with others and needed mending. He would also visit other destinations for example, the Vatican. There are pictures at the Vatican that hold prisms within them. Charles would unlock each doorway and reach the high vibrational evil within. Mary followed him there with another to close these doorways, however the vibration was so menacing that it went right through her and caused a flow of darkness. It was hard to distinguish. Like an Indiana Jones movie, Mary never forgot the fright of that experience. That feeling never left her memory. And she never experienced that feeling again!

Mt. Everest was another destination of Charles however the godly would not allow him in. His fits of rage could not be felt in holy places that are well guarded. But oh how Charles tried!

There was much time that Mary could not account for. Perhaps Charles had taken time away but Mary felt that she buried much of her real self to preserve all that was good and for fear that darkness would snatch it away. Those chords of darkness could not grab onto anything that was not there or so she thought. Mary hid her true self well, not only for survival, for preservation of her true nature. She emerged when she felt safe, unable to be touched. But this was rare. Mary was beginning to understand how Anne Frank lived. Due to being your true self meant risking being found and then all would be taken from her. Evil have ears and sight. Charles would check on her many times a day. His possessive nature and his chording would attack as though it were an hourly ritual. Like the ready men who press the bomb, he went to sleep thinking of Mary and woke up doing the same.

Kenneth came back to Mary with much information to help her. He was able to extend her life well beyond the years she was destined. We all have our gifts and he had his. He stated that all tribute to the Creator must be pure and sincere. Mary remembered that in the Bible it states that when you seek help from others instead of the God-force directly, others will give you that outcome. Knowing this fact, Mary was hesitant for any outside help, but this circumstance was all about Mary's faith and her patience in the God force.

It was discovered that many criminals possess the Asperger gene. Mary was exhausted from the day to day battle that took its toll. We amaze ourselves by our strength of endurance that we can emotionally, physically and spiritually uphold. Yet Mary discovered she had head and neck cancer. This was a contract made before this lifetime that had to do with the government. But Mary could not help but think that Charles was responsible for all.

There were those healers who would chord into you upon meeting. Their information would leave certain key points out that would have you returning to pay more monies. Mary would imagine what her life would have been like without Charles. It would have been peaceful and loving. Only Mary and the Creator knew what Mary endured.

Chapter 14

Mary's Allegiance

THE SPOOF THAT CHARLES enacted throughout his life was a control of others without them knowing. Sometimes the lame or afflicted harbor evil masters and they use the body as a vehicle to their demise. And sometimes this is seen especially in nursing homes.

Charles would laugh to himself when he played God and would alter the lives of thousands. He would never let Mary escape for Mary knew too much. Yet how could she prove all that she had seen and felt? This was the enigma.

In his eyes, he was a black magician who only knew his emotions. His presence was feared by many and revered by those who do evil deeds. His intellect was superior, as most who possess Asperger's. Mary allowed energetically to feel less superior to him, weak and naïve. In this manner he would not increase his attacks or bother Mary's family. Sometimes this worked and other times it did not.

Mary buried much of her true self waiting for herself to emerge. A family member of Charles's appeared one night to Mary. A woman with a white porcelain face and a long taffeta skirt who helped Charles gain control of the road Mary was headed on. Lies poured forth from Charles's mouth in order to save his path to Mary. His family helped him whether they believed his lies or not. She kept Mary detoured for quite some time. Mary was led astray but eventually Mary returned to her path. Charles always played the poor innocent victim when Mary was involved. It was quite the opposite. Mary never saw Charles after that first encounter at her home. Yet Charles persisted in his lies and his evil ways. Lies were well received, with the support from others.

Mary remembered what Kenneth had told her, "we only fear the Lord and no one else." And anything Kenneth spoke of that time was not half as important as that statement.

It was hard to believe that the torch of love perpetuated Charles forward when he never felt Mary's reciprocal love. Yet how could someone so evil have love in his heart? Somewhere deep down in the crevices of Mary, she felt there was a small piece of him that was good and this kept Charles ever vigilant of this idea. This toxic relationship needed to be severed. That which we do not possess, we want it even more. Mary was all that Charles was not. And he was determined to find a way to make her his own. We all are capable of love no matter on what level or on what scale we measure. And Charles was no exception!

But no one has the right to keep us prisoner, nor negate another's life by any means. And yet Charles crowned himself and dubbed himself worthy of his cause.

That pompous, arrogant soul, who thought he could get away with all he had done to Mary and others. Mary waited and became quite patient for that right moment when he was no longer continually pursuing his beloved.

Like the wolf who waited for the rabbit to pass by, Mary would not forget all that had been done to her. Trauma is not easily forgotten. For Mary turned the cheek many a time and gave Charles the chance to stop his evil ways. But can a man who has signed his life over to the Devil ever change? Yes, but not when their life is edged on by demons and reptilians. Walk tall Mary, walk tall!

Chapter 15

The Battle Waged on

EVERY DAY MARY WAS thankful for her life. And all that she had, even though it was very little. She had been stripped of all her possessions and left with a bare slate! Charles had sewn up all that she did daily to leave the past over and done with, with no return.

As for the characters in Charles's line up, they had their own peculiarities. They all marched to the conviction with societal grievances and how they were handed a raw deal in one form or another. Their telepathic union fought for justice from whomever they could live through, especially Mary. And their negative onslaught brought Mary crashing down with much disbelief and bewilderment. The once regimented life of happiness and joy was smashed and brought down to the point of forgotten hopes and dreams. And a fear overcame Mary as to what happened. Mary not only felt lost but also a death. We all must be brave in these circumstances!

Stand up for who we are despite with one or with many. And for such a long time, Mary did just that!

In the end, all go back to their home, safe and secure, and remind themselves, "it will never happen to me."

Mary found much solace in those who possessed those who could block Charles even though they were hard to find. Mary's good karma saved her from the onslaught of attacks by Charles. These attacks by law were criminal in nature and yet no one came to her rescue to imprison Charles, despite all her attempts to let them know. It was Charles that needed to be imprisoned and confined. For in jail, Mary thought Charles would not be able to perform his witchcraft, voodoo and sorcery. However through those thin walls, Charles could send his assistant energy to carry out his evil deeds. Outside of Mary's home, there were many a night that Charles would send energy via his assistant to reach her window. Energy can also be sent through wires and the computer.

In order to forget Mary's experiences, she underwent hypnosis to drown out all that happened. Hypnosis did not work. When Encountering Charles, one had to be strategic. All needed to be tightly sealed, arranged and accurate. There was no room for errors, no loopholes that Charles could find to misalign, fracture or dismember. Chaos needed to brought down to a minimum. When all could not be found by Charles, he would find a weak point in the body and try to continually hit it and thus eventually enter in the night, knees, hips and toes.

Trauma evoked can cause fear and anxiety. Once Charles paid a comrade to have Mary envision seeing her daughter held by a fireman going through intense flames. Mary was fearful and then this comrade was heard on Mary's roof making heavy steps. This then allowed Charles and his comrades to enter the body and instill fear. Such imagination!

Those that were professing to help Mary, all along were crying, "it is the end of the world," while they took Mary's monies on behalf of her protection. All, Thieves and liars. One would wonder who was worse, Charles or them. Yet a few passed the test of helping Mary. And she was so ever humble!

Mary was not always told the whole story, for fear if Mary knew the whole story from her healers, she may not want to come back. And we surely did not want that, would we!

The angel of the Lord watches over us and guides us no matter what happens and Mary believed this. She had difficulty taking hold of her situation. The belief that Jesus and the Creator were more powerful than Charles led to an awakening. No doubt would engulf her this time. She gave it all to the Creator!

All jobs Mary worked at were interfered with by Charles. The darkness not only overshadowed Mary, he used mind control on those that worked close to her. There was no escape. Mary however endured going from job to job and wondered why.

Exhausted from day to day, Mary continued onward. That what we ask for may not always have the right timing. Much sadness enveloped Mary and there were times she cried herself to sleep. Mary could not explain all that was happening to her. Again, who would believe her? The Creator heard her and kept her alive. Mary's face always looked glum and filled with heaviness. Archangel Michael was called upon. The benevolent kept her safe. Her sadness projected that of a sad clown. Others would add, "You need to see a doctor, is there anything wrong?" So Mary would explain that there was nothing wrong but she would consider seeing the doctor, just in case.

Mary's remedy was calling upon her healer. He would go deeper and deeper till some progress was made. And then for a time, Mary felt at peace with herself until the next intrusion or attack. If we are not avid meditationalists, we need to take ten minutes out of our day to practice. Mary never meditated so this became a challenge to her. It is when we connect to the divine that we are able to shield that which attacks us. The dark energies cannot ever go that high. Oh, but they will try!

If Mary was not meditating or aware that Charles or his assistant were in her higher realms, then they would hold or detour all on her path. Chanting and singing high pitches enabled him to follow all she did. When a technique would not work, he quickly changed to another method of attack. He never lost time, nor down time.

Doubt in the Creator was also played upon by Charles. Looking back and wondering if things would take place was preyed upon by him. His strength became greater when the force of evilness took precedent over Mary's doubt of the Creator's power. At any moment of doubt, Mary felt a binding forever dipped in loneliness and cyanide for her to swallow. And at this point, Charles felt he had an advantage over Mary.

Chapter 16

The Creator and Mary

TOWARDS THE END OF this battle with Charles, Mary envisioned herself as a Greek monk with headdress and all. It is by this, that Mary knew what she had actually been through and what she had endured. For no one could travel this road of darkness without spiritual guidance and endurance. And no one dare try!

The picture painted by Charles to others, was a grim fabrication of his own grievance of deep seated rejection that reached a height of unprecedented proportions. Even though Charles tried very hard to lead John down a road of decadence and decay, the darkness never reached his core. Charles and the others accessed John's ex-girlfriend, only to find their manipulative nature turn on them. These things never work. They were evil and hurtful to Mary, yet their plan failed.

Mary kept her mind occupied during this time. Every day she would run around and do whatever was needed urgently. Then the evening would come and it would be time for bed. She was under a vicious cycle when everything would repeat itself. She felt like a character whose head was buried in the present, trapped by the rhythm of her life, unable to escape. She prayed and cried many a time for Charles to let go of her and John. As the years passed, Mary learned to live with all that had been done against her, yet the anger grew.

Negative energy can be neutralized all by the right frequency. As Charles would look at your fears upon meeting, he would be able to understand what was effective. A very precise situation or crossroad repeated itself in her effective life, and time and again her feelings remained continuously trapped. There were special circumstances which caused Mary difficulties in controlling the opposite sex. It is at this juncture that she would let herself be manipulated and misled. Her intellect was fully aware of the traps prepared for her, but not to the intentions or schemes. This was a technique Charles used until Mary could find a solution. Charles was brought into this world to create chaos yet he tried so hard to fit in with others.

He developed a hard outer shell, that plotted and schemed how his defenses would trap all who decided to become his friend or come near him. The fear of being disliked and rejected caused an avalanche of rolling thunder that came crashing down upon these unsuspecting souls. Even Mary's ancestral lineage was disturbed by Charles in order to gain information about Mary's patterns of behavior. Mary's ancestors were shaken by such behavior that Mary could see in the dream state, their shocked reactions to their shaken world. There are also those of less fortunate circumstances that are able to see how well Mary was savvy in business. Mary would always wonder who was tapping into her energy and stealing her good fortune. The key here is to catch them and be able to close them off. Mary never spoke highly of such people.

Chapter 17

Charles's Tricks

IT WAS AMAZING AT all the coincidences that Mary encountered once she met Charles. A Shaman told her that studied Mu from Lemuria, that the road she lived on meant, "come and get me." And that a legion was on its way to do just that.

A healer also went around the world healing vortexes that were negative. The portal that was five miles from Mary was in a position of negativity. It reached from the Gulf of Mexico to the Bermuda Triangle. He healed it with Arch Angels and with rainbows. An individual once mentioned a "Sigil." It is a symbol that can be placed upon a picture of an individual. And angels of the light can cause a plethora of angels to bombard the individual. A small amount of your blood is smeared on a Sigil. Mary never tried this but nevertheless it sounded interesting. Mary's duality of keeping her feet on the ground in this world, while combating in the spiritual, was conflicting and chaotic. Who could understand that she was bombarded by evil doers under the command of one character, named Charles? He probably needed to take his medicine and act out his frustrations in role play with group therapy. Yet the Creator chooses those who mirror our shadow side to push us toward greater enlightenment and direction. And when we reach that point when all is said and done, the terror stops and all comes to an end.

For all the karma Charles accrued, it came back to him in sixes and nines. His road of revenge traveled behind him like a dog with a wagging tail. Charles also sought those from the other side, especially his mother. He gathered up demons, especially a large demon chained to him for protection. Yet at times, Charles felt he was only contributing to Mary's light. And he continued to fight for Mary and then against her.

Mary's love life seemed impossible. She could not feel the soul mate anymore. Charles drowned their love with all darkness, like furnaces reaching to heaven. At times he would enter qigong points in her private area and travel through a neuropathic way to her heart. In doing so, he would feel as though he were hitting her love to take a piece of what he would never have. Mary finally was able to close all portals and doorways. He would also intertwine his energy with her divine channel.

Mary pondered about why the dark energies are well formed and work as a whole? The difference is the light says how much. The faster you are well armored, the faster no one can take advantage of these truths and afflictions. There are those that can seal you that no one can touch you for one thousand dollars. Although very effective, they are void of godliness. And where were all the social workers checking on Charles? His lies and energetic blocking kept him well afloat from any intrusions into his private life. He was a free floating ball of chaos that hid under a big hoop skirt, playing the afflicted, with Asperger. If only all knew his deviousness. It is only under medication that one really would come to know Charles for who he really was. And not until then!

In the beginning, Mary was put in a well like Joseph and then put in a whale like Jonah. Charles thought that he would have some fun with Mary. Mary did not find it amusing. She was busy recuperating from this prophetic blow. Yet Mary's faith kept her ever vigilant toward the Creator. Many would contend that Mary went through a moment of illusion or hallucination. Those of spiritual sight could see Mary for her honesty without question. And these were no mere illusions! Two Shamans from different regions decided to throw Charles in the Lake of Fire. To their dismay, he survived.

A man who worked with lasers also decided to try his technique. However, despite his knowledge of such things, Charles survived after doing it twice to him. His skepticism brought much confusion to himself. "I can't understand it," he spoke, " it always works."

Chapter 18

At a Crossroad

IN CHILDHOOD IT WAS found that a demon at various developmental stages would enter Mary and be lodged into a particular organ. A man who does such studies performed his research, to find out about Mary's characteristics. Angels also visited Mary and when any disturbance from angels or demons were present, some monumental experience happened at various stages. One particular experience that stood out amongst the rest, was when a military man babysat her at the age of five. He was a friend of the family. However when he babysat her, his ill intent opened a door that Charles discovered. This door was open and led Charles to hold onto it to create adversity in Mary's life. It was merely intent, but nevertheless the damage was prevalent. Mary closed this door finally with no looking back.

As the illusionary and mesmerizing energy attacked Mary, it would be broken down at the cellular level so new programming could be introduced. Mary continued to become a new person.

At times Mary became the ghost whisperer to Charles. She would whisper to Charles in his ear that to, "forget her, she really doesn't love you." "It is time to leave her alone." Odd that Charles was doing this to Mary's soul mate. Neither listened nor took notice. Charles daily went on Mary's timeline. He foresaw that once she met her soul mate, if that happened, she and he would adopt a child. Charles made certain this would not happen. He energetically would negate this by seeing all those involved and negating this experience. His evilness worked overtime, and he prevailed.

Charles's affinity towards bugs and flying things was quite remarkable. He delved in what they call "Bat Medicine." He would enter the insect or flying insect and control its mind and energy. Once at Mary's daughter's wedding, he flew into the house as a bat, using it as a hearing device, to hear all that took place. To everyone's shock, they were running around screaming. Mary knew who it was and quickly got out her broom. On other occasions, he would become an annoying knat that would not die. He would buzz around you and then eventually try to enter your body through your ear or mouth. Wearing earphones helped with this problem. This knat would see all that Mary was doing and hear all that she said. He needed to be near her! Charles also performed sleep spells. As you were sitting or lying down, one would think at times you may be tired. Mary at first thought this but she was knocked out cold, as if she were given sodium pentothal. Charles had performed a sleep spell. This particular sleeping technique allowed Charles to enter the outside of Mary's body and chord into her. This lasted about an hour. In this manner he was able to track her energy wherever she went. This too was finally stopped. Heavy energy did not prevail!

On a different occasion, Mary felt that she was experiencing vertigo. As she woke up one morning, the room was ever spinning. Charles had placed a large vortex right at a particular point that would cause Mary to become imbalanced at the back of her head. That day, it took much time for Mary to regain her balance. All were eventually dismissed.

Mary, before she met her main healer, would work with other healers. As she were talking on the phone to the one healer, he asked Mary to stay on the phone so that his friend could listen to her condition. Mary was wise enough to understand what the healer was up to. Both were on different phones and would work in unison, as they took energy from Mary's pineal gland. Mary quickly slammed down the phone out of disgust. She felt sorry for anyone who ran into these two vampires. The pineal gland is considered the fountain of youth to some. Is this what happens with those bored with life, with nothing to do? There was a young mafia man who wanted to help Mary with a talisman. He stated that most experiences similar to hers would end in anger for time taken from their life. As time passed, he was right. Mary never saw him again nor did she take the talisman. She did not believe in them.

Devices at one time or another are also planted. As more and more past lives were removed from Mary, devices that acted as transmission for mind control, cult activity from various sources were discovered. Energies can be traced back to the source.

Whenever Charles felt he was about to be beaten, he would try harder to perform a sinister act. Mary did not want Charles to find out what she was up to, due to severe chastisement. But he did and Mary paid the price of his outrage. So Mary waited to see her main healer and all was cleared. All was taken away and new building blocks took place.

Chapter 19

The Meeting

THERE WERE TIMES THAT Charles would make Mary feel good, however this was only the rope being lent out to pull it back with greater control. He then proceeded to clamp it shut with binding.

In the beginning of Charles meeting Mary, he would enter the ground through her feet. This was stopped by placing the seals of Solomon under her feet. Many years passed and this was not permanent. Whittling her feet down, like someone using a knife to make them slimmer, was felt. It took much time to repair. Charles would continue his voodoo as the years went by.

Accidental falls and broken items would fall from shelves or places. Many prayers would be said and angels called upon daily. Charles's friend from Haiti would be contacted from time to time. This particular friend devised a way for Mary not to be able to ascend upon death, the soul would not go to the higher realms. Mary was able to distinguish all. One of Charles's assignments in this life was to defray Mary from her path. It was never Charles. It was the dark demons using Charles as a pawn. He was recruited to perform such a feat. All along, Charles thought it was he who performed such atrocities against Mary, but it was not.

Chapter 20

A Heavenly Court

CURSES, WITCHCRAFT, SORCERY, AND much more had come down from generations long ago. A Luciferian from ten generations ago, opened up the door to evil in Mary's generational family. Luciferian is defined by Wikipedia states that, "Luciferianism is a belief system that venerates the essential characteristics that are affixed to Lucifer. The tradition, influenced by Gnosticism, usually reveres Lucifer not as the Devil, but as a liberator, a guardian or guiding spirit, or even the true god as opposed to Jehovah."

Mary realized at this moment of illumination what she truly was up against! She found her life similar to Job in the Bible and came at times to terms with this reality. Yet being away from her soul mate was very hard for her to bear. And for twelve and one half years, Mary battled Charles and waited for all to stop. This was too long for anyone to bear. Yet Mary kept her faith and did not veer off her path to accept any evil that came her way. She told herself, "we cannot be afraid nor fear the future," as she persevered forward. And she was alive which was a miracle!

She could not feel her soul mate but she never gave up hope. Beyond the soul mate, the Creator waited for Mary to seek his love for him and this was finally understood by Mary. Beyond our meager existence lies a greater picture and plan that we refuse at times to acknowledge. Mary only wanted to be with her soul mate yet she was forced to listen, even though she had free will. Mary was chosen by the Creator to clear her linage for all time, clearing from today all the way back to Adam. The Creator chose this for her before her birth. For Mary was an exceptional being before the Lord and she was like no other. Nor would there ever be another Mary.

There were three holy men and one holy woman who assisted Mary in holding a Court of Heaven on her behalf. The angels, Archangels and the Creator held a spiritual court and represented all that Mary stood for.

On the other side of the court was Charles and all his demons, Luciferians. This consisted of all connected to Charles and from Mary's background. The awe reverence of the heavens, kept Mary shining in her glory. The feeling of heavenly bodies was one of long standing and love, of great magnitude. No darkness could be found or felt. Peaceful ambiance filled the courtroom that nothing could compare. On the other side of the courtroom were demons with horns, Charles and all those who were behind Charles. One of the holy men could see the Levithian, an octopus, a dragon and a white witch with yellow eyes. All came from past generations, from the beginning of time, from Mary. The biggest influence in Mary's background was the Luciferian, from ten generations past. This opened to what Mary was experiencing today. And was the foundation for all that happened to Mary, Mary's family and all relative generations from today, reaching back ten generations. To Mary's understanding, she had to keep a godly life while she combated the darkness of Charles. But now came the time to end all of this. The Court of Heaven is what was needed to be done and it took Charles by surprise. Charles thought all under his control and nothing could be further than the truth. As he held his cobra in one hand and shook his hand in another, he faced the court with fear and bewilderment. The time of torture, lies, abuse and much more, was about to come to an end.

Mary was also cleared of a Jezebel spirit. This evil spirit had been responsible for not only tearing down churches, pastors and different Christian Ministries, but it has also been responsible for breaking up marriages, friendships, companies, along with getting many people to commit cold-blooded murders and suicides.

As the Bible mentions in (Mathew 12:43), there are levels of wickedness in Satan's kingdom. As mentioned from a priest, "the Jezebel spirit is more intelligent than some of the lower ranking demons and is very good at playing head games with people." It is a total control spirit, that is very good at manipulation and getting people to do its evil bidding. Mary was also battling this from Charles.

Another spirit Charles enacted was the "Mocking Spirit." A spirit of mockery that taunts and ridicules God's work in your life. A conversation would come across Mary's brain stating, "who do you think you are?" "None of this God stuff will work for you because you are worthless!" "Do you really think anyone will listen to you?"

One point that Mary did not expect were the chords from the Underworld. There were attachments that needed to be broken. There were twenty two chords and nine hundred and eighty members in her lineage since Adam, trapped in the Underworld. As so above, as so below. There is more than one layer in the Underworld.

The Creator says you are more than good enough, you are more than a conqueror! (Roman's 8:37), God called you worthy and you can do all things through Jesus Christ who strengthens you. (Phil.4:13)

You are not rejected but adopted into the family of God's son. (Eph. 1:5) As a person mentioned to Mary, that "none of us are immune to hearing demons, but knowing the truth keeps you from listening and agreeing with their lies." Mary finally brought a crashing end to this spirit, if only in her mind! It was brought to light in the Courts of Heaven.

Mary was combating many spirits on many different levels, not only Charles and his entourage. Mary thought they were all coming from him, yet he brought them into play!

The courtroom was filled with mostly angels waiting for the final verdict to commence. This was a long awaited event that the angels patiently held in their loving embrace. It became a crossroad that was finally crossed and never to be crossed again. Finding herself here in heaven was more than she could ever want to experience. The day had finally arrived to state her case and all that she had been through. Psalm 23, "He restoreth my soul." She was in a Court of Love that predominantly ruled in the courtroom. This court also removed sabotage against Mary and her lineage.

Today the bells were ringing in heaven that called all the angels to be present. Job was present to represent telling the court, how Mary's life was similar to his. It was brought to light that Charles meshed his soul with Mary's through a demonic force that ruled him, a soul tie. Mary forgave the human but not the enemy. Many curses were brought to light regarding Mary's lineage that were from Mary's Greek heritage. Mary remembered that many who have had experiences similarly to Mary's, are classified as auditory hallucinations. However, one of the holy men asked Mary if she was Bible based. She was and then it was never mentioned again. She also mentioned she was born again.

Mary at this time was brought into light about her power over demons and the Devil. In time the Creator would reveal to her this power. Mary's power within the kingdom would be great. Mary held much more power on the other side next to the Creator.

Charles's assignment played the role the dark ones enacted, while looking for a recruit. And he took the bait. On this day, Mary would never know if his infatuation was all of his own doing or those of others, casted upon him. She did know that the demons controlling Charles were many. For Charles was a trickster, shapeshifter, court jester, when all the while he had a ferocious demon and demons behind him, leading the way of other demonic forces. The signature of the Devil was upon him. That was the true Charles! And it was also discovered that there were no beings in middle earth but only Charles. A pure fabrication, trying to control Mary. Mary truly was disheartened and shocked to find out all. He enacted all to bring not only attention to Mary, but also to bind her at that moment of acceptance.

As the gavel went down, Mary presented her case well, against Charles. The court adjourned in her favor. Charles had a restraining order placed upon him. Yet this did not hold Charles for very long. Mary was quite happy about the Court of Heaven that had helped her clear not only her lineage, but Charles. And every time she thought about her Court time, she became stronger in that bond to the Creator.

Chapter 21

So Called Friends and Healers

CONNECTED WITH HER THROUGH mutual minds, Jennifer helped her receive that which Mary was seeking. Her understanding led her to assist Mary in realms that Mary could not obtain herself. Our intent is always important. It is our gateway to receiving. Although the more we repeat experiences, the more we learn about them. Jennifer was able to lend words of wisdom that allowed Mary to understand her own way of thinking. She stated, "as long as you hold the thought that Charles has the power to trace and control, then you are preventing greater power than him from fixing the issue." "Charles cannot control another soul. Period, absolutely impossible. That is a false to fact image, and he has gone to great lengths to suggest that is the case. And you have accepted it as truth. It is not!" Mary went over and over these words to let it go deep within. She gave Mary a set of tools to understand forces that she could use. She let Mary come to know that she still held the memory construct on her hard drive. "You haven't taken it into the fires yet and transmuted the low frequency into high frequency energy essence." Jennifer reassured Mary that all doors have been closed and locked down with new locks. She mentioned, "you just need to make damned sure that you don't let him back in!"

"Perhaps your real mission is to save him. Unlike Princess Leah Organa, become Leah Skywalker, Jedi Master." "Even he is a beautiful soul that has strayed off course." Mary did not want to entertain this last thought since Charles could use this to his advantage. She did not want to even mention his name.

Jennifer had Asperger's Syndrome and was quite intelligent and most helpful. Her words echoed wisdom for quite some time. "You are doing an excellent job at taking care of your part. You are aware of what is coming in, and taking care of it." "You were caught off guard with his attack while you were asleep, but you moved on it fairly quickly. You did get an intuitive message that it was coming in, but it slipped past. Go back over the messages from the night before and you'll find it." "The Actualism founder, Russell

Schofield, called it effortless effort. It's doing by not doing. By doing all of the doing outside of time, space. Let the soul do it all. Turn over all control and permission to the spiritual being that you are, your own immortal, and let the work happen from your soul." This helped Mary a great deal. She saw the intent then let it go.

Mary remembered that the wise man and the female Shaman decided to help Charles chord Mary from her private area down to the middle of the earth, in order to ground her. By bringing this anchor of energy deep within the ground, Charles thought he would keep Mary from roaming. Mary did not find this amusing and continued on her way. Since Mary had invested much monies in her dwelling, she had to protect her home. Her home was a condo and much had been taken from her. In the middle of the night, Mary surrounded her complex with kosher salt, so that all could be safe. Even Mary found this humorous while pouring salt around a condo complex three to four times larger than her own condo, at two in the morning. Mary prayed that none of the neighbors saw her. And if they did, she would mention that she was fertilizing the soil. Her home on the corner was a beacon of light. Charles knew where she lived and would visit her home with different colored cars for five minutes outside her window. When he decided to make himself less conspicuous, he would have others survey her home with vans and other vehicles. This led to also using others as transporters of his energy to reach her window. They acted as conduits to connect his energy with Mary's. Also noises would occur in different parts of the home. All knew it was Charles. And to scare Mary, he would have sheets fly in her bedroom. This was not amusing! Charles also decided to go below Mary's residence 50ft to ground his energy. Mary found this out after someone had come to survey the land.

Yet when Mary needed to move, due to Charles, Charles traveled right behind her energetically. Mary felt trapped and decided to move again however it was very costly. At her new home, Charles appeared with shadows in and out of her home and bothered her in the night. All came to a stop when she was able to turn the situation around. Since Charles worked diligently around the clock at this point, his friends and enemies would not help him. They found him obsessed and not wanting to let go of Mary. He did not want to lose all that he had fought for, nor invested. Yet the end of this battle was soon approaching. His searching for anyone who would listen to his cries made his onslaught all the more evil and treacherous.

Witchcraft, sorcery and black magic were enacted to continue on their evil road of destruction and darkness on Mary's path. For those individuals, the heavenly nor the Underworld have no place for them. Charles needed to stand trial in the Underworld by Hades. Yet Charles would not face this till his death. And that was not very soon. However, he was fast approaching jail. The Father did not allow Charles to go unpunished. For it would be a long time before Charles would be set free. And then again many came forward to protest their injustices that they suffered on behalf of Charles. Mary decided not to pursue Charles for all that he had done. She wanted no part of all that she endured. Yet Charles would not go down easily. His plotting led him to contact a red haired woman who also performed witchcraft to help him finish what work he had started. Mary heard, "yes, I will take care of the rest, Charles." Mary then received a phone call from this woman disguised as a bill collector. Her calling led her to know who she was dealing with and an assessment was made. Mary saw through Charles's scheme and slammed the phone down. Nevertheless, she kept calling to pretend she was an authority figure. The nerve! Charles also decided to employ a woman from Haiti who did voodoo. She was an ever vigilant voodoo puppet with her candles and gyrations. Haiti, the capital of voodoo!

It was discovered from a past life that Mary participated with these two women who were centennial. However, she walked away from these practices in another life. As mentioned before, although she walked away, the darkness followed her due to the oath taken. All needed to be rooted correctly so that it would never be experienced again. Symbols and curses from grids, were removed. A layer of incantations, spells and curses, also needed to be removed from a past life. This energy was letting her know that she could not survive without their dark energy. Karmic impression upon karmic impression.

These centennials were holding a grid in a place related to Mary's past life. A tremendous darkness was released from her back that allowed Mary to breathe with much freedom. It was a very dark and heavy energy to hold Mary in this life, down. By neutralizing negative vibrations, Mary chose to do her daily clearing and her God- force energy was always constantly growing in her environment. Mary felt sick at times as she cleared all from her home, lineage and herself. Mary felt this and at times she would be sick from this but she continued onward. As in any group from our past and present day happenings, similar to

Charles's group, all go to a similar place upon death and reincarnate together in the next life time. We see this with gurus and religious groups in present day. Mary was rooted to these centennials at the earth chakra. This is an indication that Mary was connected to them from a past life. Even in the chakras at a deep level, there were symbols that could allow dark negative energies, curses and hexes in, occult activity. This is why Mary chose to clear herself using layer upon layer, to clear all not connected to the God-force. Since the chakra opens to the front and back, it was important to clear through vibration all that was in the core, all was in the spine. Accompanying all was Charles's mesmerizing, illusionary and anti-Christ energy. All were released and positive energy was integrated.

We cannot prevent anyone from sending negative energy to us, however, we can protect ourselves through prayer, singing positive vibrations, communion and understanding what vibration can remove and neutralize negative energies. Mary, through trial and error, found that heavy negative energies could be combated easily, while others needed much diligent working with each day. Poverty engrains its mark in such people who think their salvation rests in the beat of their lives. Mary and her healer were able to block all. Even though Mary never believed in such things, Mary took no chances. Charles had to make a point, the point of winning no matter at all cost.

He wanted to be master. Mary was foolish to think there was any kindness in Charles at this point. He was far too gone!

Mary also remembered from her pagan friend to write everything down. In this manner, your thoughts could not be heard or be repeated. Mary wrote down everything that was of importance so that her reflection would not be for too long. She also continued to question her thoughts, were they hers or someone else's?

Ideas or thoughts that popped into her head were snatched by Charles and his comrades from her higher level. It was as though a funnel had been placed to avert all that Mary was thinking. This was eventually resolved.

There was an energy that was attached to Charles. This energy ran like a river under Mary that was of a dark nature. It spoke of a menacing energy that stated, "If you do not align with this dark energy, you will not be permitted to any material things. We will permit you minimal survival issues, however, that will be all." Mary and her healer fought this energy and prevailed. Mary wondered if humanity faces this trial?

Chapter 22

Love at Last

UNTIL MARY COULD SOLVE all that Charles was throwing at her, daily and hourly, her life persisted to be chaotic and confused. She was always wondering what would happen next. Not until every morsel of energy was configured and returned to a normality, would Mary find peace in her life. Mary consistently took every day anew and attacked it as though the God-Force gave her another day. Charles's love for Mary grew angrier and angrier each day. He wanted to hurt and harm her. It became evident that only his assistant was loyal to the end. It also became evident that he was under mind control and possession by Charles, to follow all his commands. He was searching for power and became dazzled by the power Charles possessed. Yet his assistant was not possessed by demons behind him, despite commands executed. There was hope that his assistant could change, but only if Charles disappeared from his life. Charles did not possess any power since the male Shaman stripped him of all, except his dark soul. It was his threatening demeanor behind him, that threatened others, through fear and servitude.

Mary could not understand that if all decided to break away, why did they not try? Their seed of evilness did not allow their soul from the never ending loop of darkness and start a new life. Like a forgotten soldier in a fable, Mary pushed forward, despite all that had been done to her. No matter how far she was led astray, the road to freedom, never was diverted, it was just postponed. That guiding light led the way. It talks to us and we must adhere to the call. We are free to be who we want to be. Once in the game you can never retreat. The chess game requires a move, backward or forward.

After meeting her soul mate, their humor over Charles found a place on the shelf, only to be mentioned for what they both endured. Mary and her soul mate learned a great deal about themselves and also what they could endure without each other. As one spoke, the other finished the other's sentence. Mary came to appreciate the little things, when all was taken away and destroyed. It is at this point she discovered the important things in her life, much more than before. Her view of the world changed and yet she never gave up hope. Her forgiveness of others grew and was seen through a kaleidoscope of colors. Her panoramic view of hope and understanding widened. This was a spiritual battle that lasted twelve and a half years, that allowed Mary to see who was really in charge. Mary's life never turned out as she had wanted but she knew her life would never be repeated in any other lifetime. Her life lessons were well learned! Mary's life was truly tested beyond measure but she always marched forward with diligence and perseverance.

No matter how far she was led astray, the road back home never was diverted. That guiding light led the way. It talks to us and we must adhere to the call. The road to freedom was a long winding road and Mary faced it with much courage and love in her heart with the Creator's assistance. Obviously, no one knows the absolute truth, but Mary sought it all her life. It became her quest because of her great open-mindedness. Her quest for absolute truth led her to become a holder of great wisdom till the end. Mary fought every attachment, past, present and in the future. For Charles diligently worked on her time line, putting in holds, negation and alterations, well into the future. That was his control, his humor. Mary on the other hand was well aware of his interferences and would consult with others to find all. All eventually were gone, all were never to return! Get along little doggie, get along. As for the others behind Charles, who followed all his commands, all continued on their path to do evil. Charles's imprint left a heavy mark upon their souls, never returning to normalcy. They continued on their evil ways, looking at themselves in their mirrors, obsessing over their bleak existence. They hid from their own lies, trying to substantiate their misgivings and all that took place with Mary. Their existence, was looking over their shoulders to find only Charles trying to pull their energy, and use their power. As for Charles's assistant, he awoke to find a new being. The spell placed upon him by Charles, was broken. He eventually returned to be himself again, for whoever that was. Charles tried very hard to hold onto him, however, the assistant decided that Charles was no longer his idol. And so, he continued on his own path, whether good or evil.

The so called Holy man that Charles had worked through, continued on his evil ways. He could not pull himself back to his righteous ways. He continued on his deceitful path, professing lies and pretending all was well with the world. All would eventually see through who he truly was, an imposter. For the dark energies made folly of his grave pathetic advice and his camouflaged kindness. Yet, he survived because he duped all with his kind words. It took time for Mary to digest all that was done to her, however, she arose with a greater understanding of what took place and with those around her. She corrected facets about herself that could not have been done without Charles, even though by unconventional means. Mary became a new person. Understanding how our world evolves and moves, is very precious indeed! New doors beckoned Mary to be open once Charles had moved on. The solution was deep, deep in Mary that painstakingly took Mary layer upon layer to discover. Deep within the chakras, in her spine, was the key to her freedom. Charles had buried it deeply, to always have this security with him. Once finally discovered, the road to freedom had arrived! The only hardship that lay before Mary was that she could never retrieve that time again and this was most unforgiving. For the wake of what Charles disturbed, took time to repair and heal from all trauma and chaos. As time goes by, forgiveness needed to be reached. As for the others, well, they were not thought about ever again. They were thought of as pawns that delved into paths of low frequency who were misguided souls.

There was no time for sadness nor misgivings. Mary was too busy being happy with her soul mate. She was granted the privilege to finally meet him and the dream was realized. Despite Charles, her soulmate needed healing. He would eventually be free from Charles but this took time. John was suffering from mind control and triggers that were placed within him so Charles could connect with him. In this manner his attachment would be through Mary's soulmate. All had to be healed, all of Mary's family, from all intrusions, whether they would listen to Mary or not. No portal, doorway, tear or entrance was kept open on every level or dimension. Charles would be forever plotting on how to get back in to Mary's life with whoever Mary would know or encounter. His obsession was ever threatening, however, Mary was ever vigilant.

The dichotomy of evil and obsession would never die with Charles. Even those who did not believe Charles was capable of such atrocities, Mary was there to show them an old movie called, "Bell, Book and Candle," with Jimmy Stewart. Through Mary's efforts and explanations, she would profess her freedom to others. Those that would listen and understand, took note of all she said.

Mary brought many to the feet of the cross. And she would never forget Charles and all she had learned. We all move forward, despite that which tries to keep us behind. Mary was then forever spreading her truth despite lies and attacks from others who were jealous or spouted that she needed to pay for her forefathers, who had done evil to others. There will always be these types of people who through lack of understanding have no other recourse but to say such things. Mary forgave these types of people, since their scope of intelligence was limited. The time it took them to form their opinions, Mary felt they could have helped her, but this was all wishful thinking.

After the mesmerizing and illusionary energy lifted for all time, all that remained was a three ring circus, Charles, the trickster and the many demons behind him and the other circus, Charles, the Shaman and the wise man. For she learned that the God-force wanted her by his side, to fight from the other side for glory and heroism. She was here on earth to prove her loyalty to the Creator and gain her freedom for all time. The Creator had a plan for her and eventually she reached it.

Her healer gave her these words to follow and reread whenever she wondered about the darkness. "Dark force energy blocks our energy channels and

reroutes our energy system to connect with the grids
that connect us to the dark source, the Evasion energy,
which is in a parallel universe to ours. All dark force
energies and entities come out of this dark source.
Children are born with dark force interference. We
must wake up out of our illusion, free ourselves of
all dark influence and interference, and align with
the Creator. We created dark force energy when we
naively misused our God given powers to create and
distorted our energy. "Giving energy to our reflections
in our original shadow imprints." Mary thought the
pure and undifferentiated power of creation itself,
where ultimate knowledge and oblivion unified, could
possibly be true as they were envisioned.

Mary returned to her love and happiness within
herself, before she met Charles. She returned to
work and lived with her soul mate with much more
understanding. For Mary was not only working for
those she loved, but for humanity. Her freedom set
free all those that feared to fight for their beliefs. And
the Creator helped her attain that goal. She was so
ever thankful and humble. She was at peace with the
Creator. The book about this little doggie was never
thought of again nor opened. Her mind played the
song by Peggy Lee, "Is that all there is?" No, there
is much more unseen and untold.

CPSIA information can be obtained
at www.ICGtesting.com
Printed in the USA
LVHW091059180120
644098LV00005B/18/J